Life and WORK
SKILLS
RULE O.K?

SONNY JOE
AND THE
RINGDOM RHYMES

D1425874

fran

Sonny Joe....s Dad

Mike Mac

First published in Great Britain in 1992
by HarperCollins Publishers Ltd
Text © Mike McCartney 1992
Illustrations © Graham Philpot 1992
author photo: Mike Collopy

A CIP record for this title is available from the British Library
·This book is set in Goudy and Caslon Open
Printed and bound in Great Britain

Sonny Joe
and the
Ringdom rhymeS
Mike McCartney

Illustrated by
Graham Philpot

HarperCollins*Publishers*

Born in Liverpool in 1944, Mike McCartney was part of
the famous 60's 'Merseybeat' era. While his brother, Paul,
became a Beatle, Mike was a member of Scaffold, who had
a number one single in the charts with *Lily the Pink*. As
well as writing and making music, Mike is a well-respected
photographer who exhibits all over the world. He still lives
in Liverpool today with his wife, Rowena, and six children.

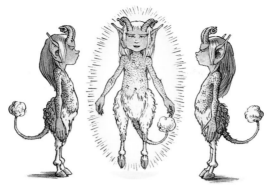

INTRODUCTION

When I first started writing this book, I was a down to earth, rational grown-up. But while I was writing I not only became involved with animals and birds and insects – but also with fairy beings. I'm not saying that this story has affected me in any way – but when I now mow the lawn, particularly round the climbing frame, I can't help giving a little 'mind-speak...' "Get out of the way of my flymo..." to certain unseen beings – just in case!

Graham Philpot has brought my Ringdom characters to life with his brilliant pen, ink and watercolour illustrations, and given them hidden depths. Look out for some very unusual little faces on bedposts and strawberries and peeping out of hedgerows.

I hope you enjoy Sonny Joe as much as me and my family have done. But a final warning – don't start writing children's stories, it's bad for your elf!

See you inside

Mike McCarthy

PS. *"Sonny and Dwarfauns caught up in Time, yours forever in Ringdom Rhyme."*

CHAPTER 1

Mr and Mrs Joe and Mary Jones, having always worked hard, could now afford to move from their run-down terraced house in the city out to the countryside. With them went their two boys; Sonny Joe Jones, his younger brother, Joshua Jones and the family pet, Harry the Girl Dog.

The house they moved to, called Sunset Cottage, was small but comfortable. The garden was large and sprawling and in the middle was an old climbing frame. All around the garden were fields belonging to a nearby farm.

At one side of the cottage the fields led down to the meandering River Pool, which flowed into the Mare Sea. On the other side, beyond the farm, the fields stretched away to a thick belt of trees, which was known as Dam Woods.

So many birds and animals visited the garden of Sunset Cottage that it was difficult to name them all: blackbirds, song thrushes, woodpeckers, robins, and owls as well as hedgehogs, moles, field mice, rabbits, bats. Now and then

even a badger or a fox crept in as dusk was falling when they could almost be mistaken for a trick of the twilight.

Mother, Father and baby Joshua Jones were happy in their new home. Sonny Joe, though, was not. He was eight years old, and badly missed the dirty old city where he had grown up. Most of all, he missed his friends. The countryside, to him, was boring.

If Mum said, "Look at those butterflies, Sonny Joe, just look at all the beautiful markings on their wings," he would say in a bored kind of way, "Yeah, but they keep flying off."

This attitude of Sonny Joe's worried Mr and Mrs Jones. They had hoped that the peace and tranquillity of the countryside might calm him down as he had picked up lots of bad habits in the city. But it didn't seem to be having any effect at all. Now and again he even played truant from his new school. His parents were worried that he might even run back to his old friends in the city.

One warm, sunny day, as they thought of all these things, Father Joe and Mother Mary watched Sonny Joe as he darted madly around their new garden, trying to catch butterflies. He kept missing them – until he hit on the bright idea of using his school blazer as a net. After stalking one particularly beautiful Peacock Eye butterfly all around the garden, he caught it as it landed in the centre of the climbing frame, with a full stretched flying tackle from the bottom rung of the frame.

Slowly and carefully he folded back his blazer until he could see a wing of the trapped insect. He glanced back to make sure his parents weren't watching. When he saw that they were, he pretended to pick flowers, and gave them a reassuring wave. When they waved back, he grinned to himself. "Fooled 'em," he muttered.

Sonny Joe looked back at the flattened butterfly and decided that before tearing off its wings he'd first rub off its powdery peacock-eye markings. He took the insect between his fingers, completely unaware that someone *else* was watching him.

Two tiny, Dwarfaun Fairy Beings had witnessed everything from the apple tree at the end of the garden. They knew exactly what Sonny Joe was up to. Unable to bear the butterfly's screams, they flew across to protest.

"Stop it!" they shouted. "Stop hurting the butterfly."

But Sonny Joe could neither hear nor see them so he just carried on.

"It's no use, Dwarfaun Gabrial," cried one of the little creatures. "We shall have to unbend his vision, then he'll see us."

"But Dwarfaun Heronimous, we cannot let him see us. That is strictly against Ringdom Rules," said Gabrial, aghast.

"I know but there isn't time to call Mandwarf." Heronimous said anxiously. "If we don't do something right now, that poor butterfly will die." As he spoke he began to peel the protective silver cloth from their Rhymestone. Then they both closed their eyes, and chanted a Ringdom Rhyme in harmony:

"Eeny Meeny Macaraca,
Alabaca Turiac…a breath of Fresh Air
The Sap of a Tree,
Let the Human Being…SEE!"

Instantly Sonny Joe looked up from the torture to find a dazzling intensity of light all around him. Somewhere near his feet was a strange, insistent, squeaking. He looked down, and then rubbed his eyes in total amazement.

Standing there were two, tiny, baby-faced people, with smooth, light-olive skins and piercing blue eyes. The top half of their bodies was covered in a sparkling, silvery material and tiny, ram-like horns protruded through their long, blond hair. Their lower halves were covered with thick matted hair and their feet looked like horses' hooves. They even had tails like a donkey, except that they ended in fluffy white rabbit bobtails.

Sonny Joe was speechless. Though the Dwarfauns were squeaking away for all they were worth, Sonny Joe could not understand a word they were saying.

"It's no good, Hero," said Dwarfaun Gabrial, "we've shown ourselves to him, but he still can't hear us."

"He can hear us all right, Gabby," Heronimous replied. "He's just too ignorant to understand."

"Do you think he'd understand mind-speak?" Gabrial asked.

"I was just about to try that," Heronimous answered, cross that he hadn't in fact thought of it first. Mind-speak was the way the Dwarfauns communicated with all the animals, birds and plants who inhabited their Ringdom. Staring into Sonny Joe's cold, green eyes, Heronimous slowly and deliberately thought the words he wanted to say.

Sonny Joe shook his head in disbelief as the words, "Stop that immediately! Can't you hear the poor butterfly's screams?" popped into his head.

He looked at the butterfly still trapped in his hand, and then back at the two angry little people at his feet. "I must be going bonkers," he said. "I'm not only seeing things, I'm hearing them as well."

"You're not going bonkers," the voice in his head told him irritably. "This is what we call mind-speak. We invented it so that animals, and lesser mortals such as yourself, could understand us. So, will you kindly release the butterfly you are holding immediately, otherwise I shall put you under a spell and turn you into something you won't enjoy."

"You and whose army?" Sonny Joe blustered back. "You can't hurt me. You're not real. I don't believe in you!" And he started deliberately to tear the butterfly's wings, forcing a last, weak, pitiful cry from the exhausted insect.

The Dwarfauns wasted no time. Tucking their tails underneath the Rhymestone, they held each other's hands in a circle above the magic stone and chanted in harmony a much more powerful Ringdom Rhyme...

"Eeny Meeny Macaraca,
Alabaca Turiac…a tongue of an Ant,
A tail of a Whale,
Human turn into…a SNAIL!"

CHAPTER 2

Time, in the human sense, stood still and in the bat of an eye the tall boy was now a small, slimy snail at the feet of the Fairy Beings.

"Ooer!" thought Sonny Joe, staring up in alarm at the huge creatures. "They've done it. They've changed me into a snail! I only hope Mum and Dad were still watching."

But they weren't. They were busy with a crying baby Josh.

Meanwhile in the long grass below the climbing frame, Dwarfaun Heronimous was giving Sonny Joe Snail a stern lecture. "Let this be a lesson to you, you're a snail now, and a snail you will remain until we think you have learnt your lesson."

"You can't do this to me!" screeched Sonny Joe. "How dare you!"

"Count your lucky stars," Heronimous snapped, as he strapped the wounded butterfly to his back, and the two of them turned to go.

"You can't leave me like this!" Sonny Joe squealed. "Come back!"

But the two Dwarfauns took no notice of him.

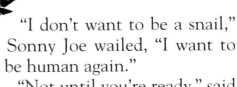

"I don't want to be a snail," Sonny Joe wailed, "I want to be human again."

"Not until you're ready," said the Dwarfauns, rapidly disappearing into the distance.

Sonny Joe was completely alone.

"When I'm ready?" he thought. "What does that mean? I'm going home. Mum and Dad will get me out of this mess." And as he started the long, slithery trek through the giant blades of grass he thought, "I hope this is just a dream. It had better be, or somebody is going to pay for it when I get back to being a boy again."

Suddenly, without warning, a large, black and white magpie swooped down on Sonny Joe. Gripping his snail shell with its claws, the magpie carried him over to the concrete pavement in front of the house. Sonny Joe shrunk back inside his shell for safety.

The magpie began to smash the snail shell repeatedly against the rock-hard concrete. Inside the shell, Sonny Joe quaked with terror, as he saw tiny cracks starting to appear. He'd never been so scared in his life.

As Sonny Joe's very life was being threatened in the garden, Mary and Joe Jones were having tea with Joshua inside the house. Outside they could hear an irritated tap-tapping.

"Go and see who that is, will you, Joseph. It might be Sonny Joe playing, and it's time he came in for his tea," said Mary.

Opening the window Father Joe saw the magpie smashing a snail against the concrete path.

"Hey!" he shouted.

Afraid of the human, but reluctant to give up its tasty escargot meal, the magpie kept hold of the snail in its beak and tried to fly off. But Sonny Joe was large and slippery and the bird simply couldn't hold onto him. Down...down he fell, landing on the path with an almighty CRACK! Sonny Joe's new home shattered and fell from his back.

Joe looked at the plight of the poor, defenceless snail, and saw that the magpie in the apple tree was ready to swoop down for the kill. He shouted "Shoo!" and waved his arms. At that, the magpie flapped off in search of an easier prey.

Without his protective shell, Sonny Joe felt horribly exposed and afraid, but glad at least that he was within sight of his father.

"Dad! Dad!" he shouted desperately, "It's me, Sonny Joe!" But Father Joseph couldn't hear him, and closing the window said, "It wasn't Sonny Joe, Mother. It was just a bird trying to eat a snail, but I've frightened if off now."

Sonny Joe Snail shivered all alone on the cold, bare concrete. "They don't even know it's me. What am I going to do?" he said as large tear drops sploshed to the ground.

It was starting to grow dark and cold. Sonny Joe began to slither towards an inviting crack in the house wall. "I wouldn't mind," he sniffed, "but I'm not even a proper snail any more. I'm an ugly slug!"

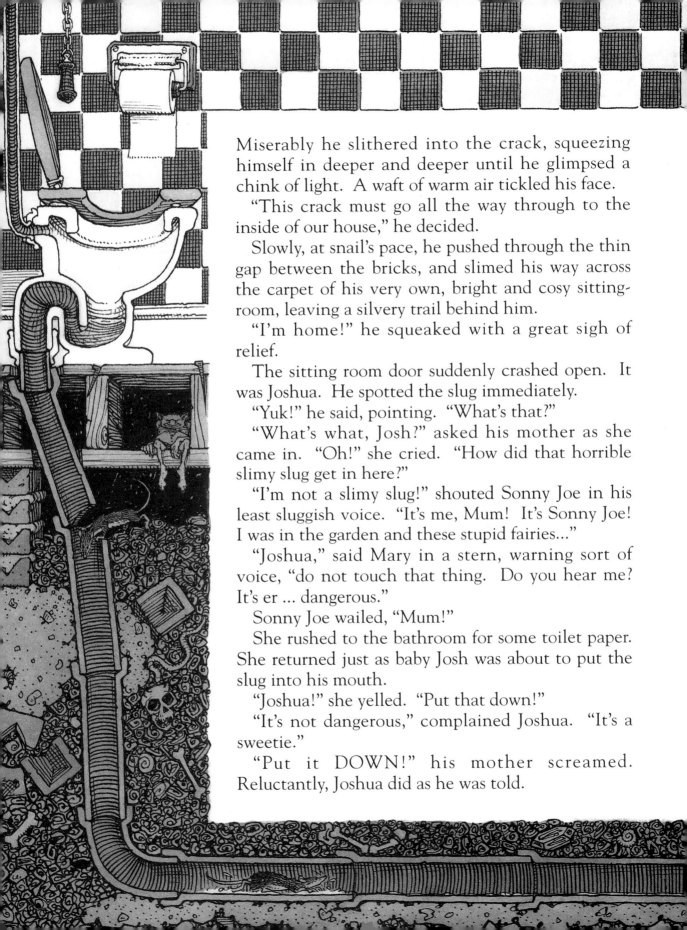

Miserably he slithered into the crack, squeezing himself in deeper and deeper until he glimpsed a chink of light. A waft of warm air tickled his face.

"This crack must go all the way through to the inside of our house," he decided.

Slowly, at snail's pace, he pushed through the thin gap between the bricks, and slimed his way across the carpet of his very own, bright and cosy sitting-room, leaving a silvery trail behind him.

"I'm home!" he squeaked with a great sigh of relief.

The sitting room door suddenly crashed open. It was Joshua. He spotted the slug immediately.

"Yuk!" he said, pointing. "What's that?"

"What's what, Josh?" asked his mother as she came in. "Oh!" she cried. "How did that horrible slimy slug get in here?"

"I'm not a slimy slug!" shouted Sonny Joe in his least sluggish voice. "It's me, Mum! It's Sonny Joe! I was in the garden and these stupid fairies..."

"Joshua," said Mary in a stern, warning sort of voice, "do not touch that thing. Do you hear me? It's er ... dangerous."

Sonny Joe wailed, "Mum!"

She rushed to the bathroom for some toilet paper. She returned just as baby Josh was about to put the slug into his mouth.

"Joshua!" she yelled. "Put that down!"

"It's not dangerous," complained Joshua. "It's a sweetie."

"Put it DOWN!" his mother screamed. Reluctantly, Joshua did as he was told.

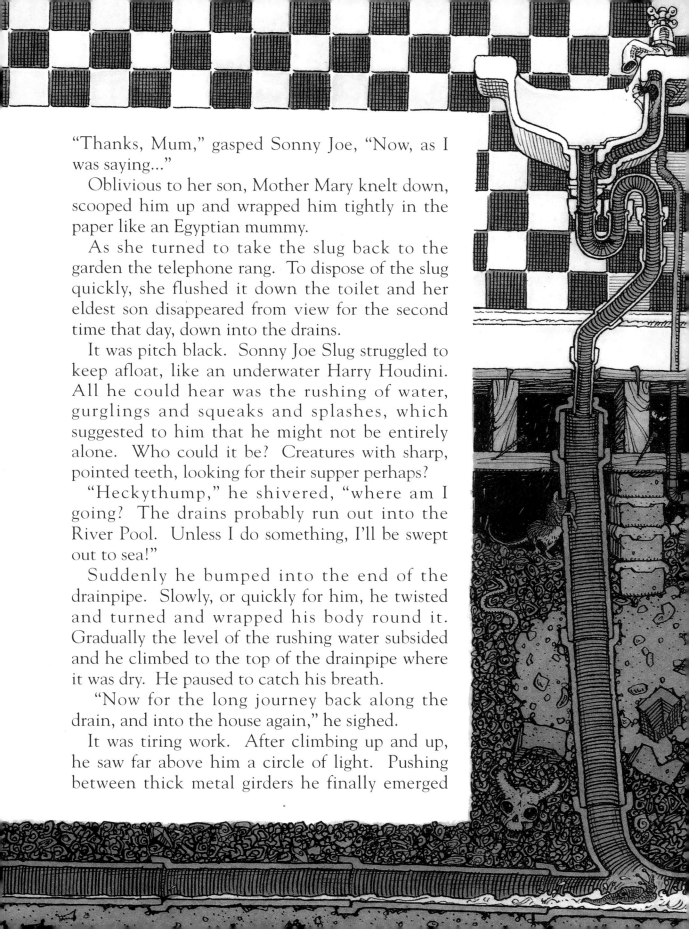

"Thanks, Mum," gasped Sonny Joe, "Now, as I was saying..."

Oblivious to her son, Mother Mary knelt down, scooped him up and wrapped him tightly in the paper like an Egyptian mummy.

As she turned to take the slug back to the garden the telephone rang. To dispose of the slug quickly, she flushed it down the toilet and her eldest son disappeared from view for the second time that day, down into the drains.

It was pitch black. Sonny Joe Slug struggled to keep afloat, like an underwater Harry Houdini. All he could hear was the rushing of water, gurglings and squeaks and splashes, which suggested to him that he might not be entirely alone. Who could it be? Creatures with sharp, pointed teeth, looking for their supper perhaps?

"Heckythump," he shivered, "where am I going? The drains probably run out into the River Pool. Unless I do something, I'll be swept out to sea!"

Suddenly he bumped into the end of the drainpipe. Slowly, or quickly for him, he twisted and turned and wrapped his body round it. Gradually the level of the rushing water subsided and he climbed to the top of the drainpipe where it was dry. He paused to catch his breath.

"Now for the long journey back along the drain, and into the house again," he sighed.

It was tiring work. After climbing up and up, he saw far above him a circle of light. Pushing between thick metal girders he finally emerged from the plug hole of the wash basin in the bathroom.

"Oh no!" he thought. "What if Mum sees me and throws me down the loo again?!"

Desperately he searched for somewhere to hide. He spotted an almost empty toothpaste tube. "Just the place," he thought and slimed his way across to it, turned round, tail first and squeezed himself in through the narrow opening. And just in time! Hardly had he managed to get inside the tube, when the door opened and his mother came in with Joshua.

"Bedtime, Joshy," she cooed. "But where on earth is Sonny Joe? Let's clean our teeth, then I'll give him another call."

Too late, Sonny Joe realised what he had done as he felt his mother pick him up. The tube began to press around him. He braced himself and pushed back with all his strength, resisting the force that wanted to squeeze him out through that narrow opening.

"Must be getting to the end of the tube," Mary said. "Hold my brush right there, Josh, so I can squeeze the toothpaste out onto it."

Toothpaste oozed and squirted past Sonny Joe, and he started to slide towards the opening of the tube. With both hands Mary rolled up the tube into a tight flattened strip.

"Ooer!" he thought. "Here I go...o...o...OH!"

And with a sudden rush, he slid uncontrollably out of the tube and onto the bristles of her toothbrush.

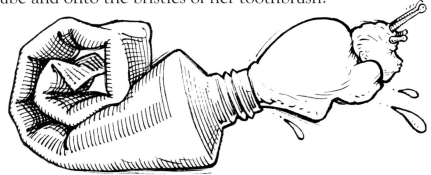

"There!" his mother said, and because he
was covered in toothpaste Mary did not
notice what was on her toothbrush!

"Now, Josh," he heard her say as she took
the brush, "watch me carefully."

Sonny Joe floated upwards on the toothbrush. Her open
mouth loomed towards him...suddenly she spotted the slug.

Father Joe was in the kitchen feeding Harry the Girl
Dog, when the scream filled the house. Dropping the box
of Dognuts, he dashed to the bathroom.

"Good heavens!" Joe cried. "What's going on?"

"My m-m-m-m-m-mouth!" wailed Mary.

Harry the Girl Dog followed Joe and joined in excitedly,
"Woof! Woof!"

"Your mouth?" Joe repeated, "what's wrong with your
mouth?" as he prized it open, and, rather like a tamer
putting his head in the lion's mouth, peered inside.

Mary stuttered, "It was n-n-nearly in my MOUTH!"

"WHAT was nearly in your mouth?" Joe asked,
bewildered.

"WOOF! WOOF!"

"Look! Under the washbasin where I threw it! A...a
sssSLUG! It was in the toothpaste. I nearly brushed my
TEETH with it!!"

Joe could hardly believe his ears. "A slug?" He bent
down to examine the blob that clung to the toothbrush.
"How on earth did it get into the toothpaste?" he asked.

"I don't care," screamed Mary, " but throw it in the
garden, then put down some slug powder. The things are
coming in through every nook and cranny."

"Certainly, dear," Joe said calmly, and taking hold of the
toothbrush, strode outside, and flung it up into the air.

"But Da-a-a-a-a-d..." Sonny Joe yelled as he left the house for the third time that day. Finally, parting company from his rocket brush, he fell down - SPLAT - into the middle of the climbing frame.

"Oh, you're back again, are you?" a not very friendly voice piped up next to him.

Shaking his head to stop seeing stars, Sonny Joe looked round and saw the two Dwarfauns looking down at him.

"Have you learnt your lesson yet?" Dwarfaun Gabrial asked.

"Lesson!" Sonny Joe shouted. "What lesson?"

"If you need to ask," Gabrial told him, "it means you can't have done."

"Now listen, you two grotty little pint-sized pixies," Sonny Joe exploded, forgetting that he was smaller than they were. "I've nearly been eaten by a bird, drowned down a drain, and almost launched into space by my own father! I've had enough, so you can say one of your stupid rhymes and get me out of this mess RIGHT NOW!"

"Certainly," Heronimous winked at Gabby.

Tucking under their tails, the two Fairy Beings joined hands over their Rhymestone and chanted in harmony:

21

"Eeny Meeny Macaraca,
Alabaca Turiac...a Crocodile's Mouth
Opening wider and wider,
Human turn into...a SPIDER!"

CHAPTER 3

Sonny Joe felt very peculiar. His body was changing shape, parts of him were getting fatter, other parts of him were becoming thinner, and eight long hairy legs were growing out of him.

"Oh this isn't fair!" he wailed, and stamping several of his spindly legs in a tantrum, he almost toppled over. "I want to go back to being a boy again."

"Why?" Heronimous asked bluntly, "so that you can go around torturing butterflies?"

"I won't!" Sonny Joe cried. "Honest Injun. I promise." He would have said anything to make them believe him. He had, however, forgotten that they could read his thoughts.

"You're only saying that," Gabrial told him. "You don't really mean it."

"I do!" wailed Sonny Joe, distraught at being found out.

"No, you don't," Heronimous told him. "Little boys who tear wings off butterflies grow up to be big men who do even worse things: mankind is destroying the planet."

"Well, if nature's so wonderful," Sonny Joe complained, "how come that magpie was trying to eat me when I was a snail? I'd say that was pretty nasty."

"That's called keeping the balance," Gabrial answered. "And that's what you humans don't seem to understand. Every single plant and creature in the whole of this world depends on the balance of nature being maintained, and if it isn't, eventually everything, including *mankind*, will come to an end. Just like a bird eating a snail."

Sonny Joe didn't fully understand them, but started to glimpse the lessons they were trying to teach him.

"Suppose I promise not to do any of those things," he said. "Can I be a boy again?"

"Not until we're sure that you mean it," Heronimous told him.

"Anyway," Gabrial chipped in, "it's not our decision any more. It's up to Mandwarf."

"Who's Mandwarf?"

"He's our superior," Gabrial replied.

"Can I see him?" Sonny Joe pleaded.

"He'll see you when he's ready," Heronimous answered. "Or, more to the point, when he thinks *you* are ready."

"Have fun being a spider," Heronimous called back, as they rose into the air.

"Fun?" Sonny Joe yelled after them. "How do spiders have fun?"

"You tell us," Heronimous replied. "But there is one thing you might as well know. It's absolutely no use trying to talk to adult humans, they'll never hear you. But if you think your thoughts as hard as you can, a young child might understand you."

And then they were gone.

"There's only one young child around here and that's my cheeky little brother," thought Sonny Joe. "Let's hope he can understand me."

And off he set on his eight spindly legs through the giant elephant grass.

* * *

Mary pulled the bedclothes up around Josh and bent to kiss him goodnight.

"Can you leave my red and green toadstool light on?" Josh asked.

"Why?" his mother said gently. "You know there's nothing to be afraid of in the dark."

"Yes, there is, there's monsters in the dark," Joshua replied wide-eyed.

"No there aren't," his mother said soothingly. "We've had this conversation before, you know there are no monsters."

"There are!" Josh insisted. "They come out to frighten me when you turn the light off."

"All right, we'll leave it on then," his mother said. "Just for tonight. But you've got to start learning to sleep in the dark like a big boy, haven't you, sweetheart? Night, night, don't fright, bed bugs won't bite," and she left the room.

Josh turned over and stuck his thumb in his mouth. Just as he was about to drop off to sleep, he had the feeling that someone was watching him. He blinked and raising his head, slowly revolved it like a submarine periscope to peer into the dark corners of the room.

At first there was not a sound or flicker of a movement. But out of the corner of his eye he caught sight of something at the far end of the ceiling above his bed. He stared deep into the shadows...and began to shiver with fright...stepping into the light was a great, big, hairy... spider!

Slowly the spider lowered itself from its web, on an invisible thread, coming lower and lower. It was aiming straight for his uncovered feet. Too frightened to move, Josh lay there, with beads of sweat breaking out all over his

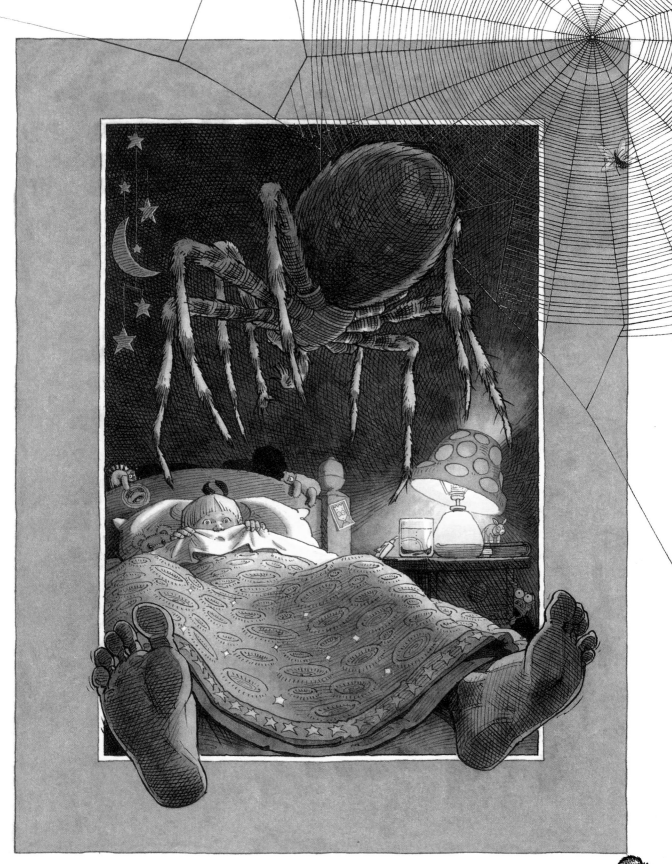

body. He could feel the blood draining from his face.

Ten centimetres away from Josh's bare feet the spider stopped. And there it hung, staring menacingly at him over the lunar landscape of his bedclothes.

"Hya, kid," the spider said, using mind-speak.

Josh was too astonished to do anything. Where had that voice come from? It sounded just like Sonny Joe.

"Hey, come on, it's only me," the voice said. "Look."

And before Josh's disbelieving eyes, the spider spun itself round on its thread, with all its legs sticking out... "Wheee!"

"Go away!" Josh squeaked.

"Why?" the voice said. "Don't you recognise me? It's me. Sonny Joe."

"You're not!" Josh said. "You're a great, big, hairy spider monster!"

"There are no such things as monsters," the spider told him.

"There are!" said Josh indignantly. "And you are not my brother. You don't look anything like him."

"That's because some rotten fairies put me under a spell," the spider explained.

"Don't believe you," Josh declared, "and my brother doesn't believe in fairies."

"He does now," the spider said. "Look," he continued, "will you believe me if I prove that I'm Sonny Joe?"

"How?" Josh said.

"I'm going to do what Sonny Joe likes doing to you when he's feeling mean or whenever you've been a pest."

"Like what?" asked Josh hesitantly.

The spider plopped gently onto his bare toes. "I'm going to tickle-torture you," he declared. And with all his furry legs, he started to tickle between, and under, and all across the soles of Josh's feet.

Josh kicked his legs madly and started to squeal and laugh all at once. "Stop it! Stop it! I'm ticklish."

"You're not tickLISH... you're tickLOTS," said the spider as he carried on tickling and tickling with all eight of his furry and not at all scary legs. Josh thrashed around in his bed laughing and crying and squealing, loving and hating every second of it!

"Stop it! Stop it! Ha-ha! He-he! Ho-ho! Please..." And, clutching his ribs with both hands, he fell CRASH BONK right out of his bed and onto the floor, taking most of the bedclothes with him.

"Now do you believe me?" the spider asked from the foot of the bed. Josh, his laughter and tears slowly subsiding, began to untangle the sheets.

"Yes," he said. "Please don't tickle me any more."

"Okay, but who am I?" the spider demanded.

"You're my big brother Sonny Joe, who's been turned into a Tickle-Spider by the fairies."

"Right," said Sonny Joe, "and you're just a cry-baby who's afraid of the dark, aren't you?"

"No, I'm not!" Joshua said indignantly, "as long as there aren't any monsters."

"Take it from me, there are NO monsters," said Sonny Joe Spider.

"I don't mind not having my red and green light on then," said Josh, feeling tremendously brave.

"Good, now listen, you've got to help me," said Sonny Joe urgently.

Suddenly the bedroom door opened and there, casting a long shadow in from the landing, was their father.

"Hello young man," he said, "I thought I heard a thud. What are you doing out of bed?"

"I fell out," Josh answered. "Sonny Joe was tickling my feet, and he made me fall out of bed."

He pointed to the spider still perched on the tail board of his bed. Joe came across to investigate.

"My, he's a big one, isn't he?" he said, as he spotted the spider by the light of the toadstool lamp. "And he's Sonny Joe, is that right?"

"Yes," Josh assured him, with wide, serious eyes. "The fairies turned him into a Tickle-Spider," said Josh, "but he can talk."

"I see." Joe nodded seriously. "Well, he's not very safe in here, is he? He'd be much happier in the garden."

"Here we go again!" thought Sonny Joe.

"No, Daddy, please," said Josh, "I want him to stay. Couldn't I keep him in a jam jar or something?" Josh asked.

"That's a bit cruel?" Dad said. "I'm not sure Sonny Joe would like being shut up in a jam jar all the time."

"Oh, I don't know," thought Sonny Joe. "I can think of worse places to be."

"He wouldn't mind, Daddy," Josh eagerly told his father. "He just said so."

"Did he really?" his dad laughed. "Well, Josh, I still think it would be kinder to let him go outside."

So saying, Joe took out a half empty matchbox from his waistcoat pocket and, before Josh or Sonny Joe had properly realised what he was doing, he scooped up his elder son inside it.

"Don't squash him," Josh begged.

"I won't," his father assured him, and going to the door he asked, "shall I leave your light on, baby?"

"Don't mind," Josh said, thinking of his conversation with his brother. "All right then. You can switch if off."

"There's my BIG boy," said his dad. And, blowing young Josh a kiss, he switched off the light and carried his eldest son out of the bedroom, securely imprisoned in the matchbox, heading for the garden.

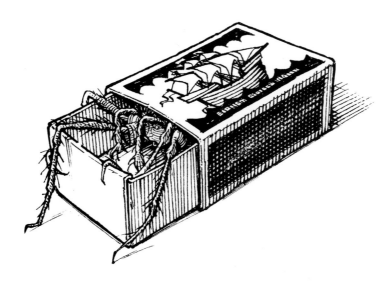

CHAPTER 4

"Well done," Heronimous managed.

"What for?" Sonny Joe asked, astonished to be hearing any praise from his giant Dwarfaun tormentors.

"You helped Josh to stop being afraid of the dark," Gabrial told him.

"Did I?" Sonny Joe said, a bit surprised.

"See? I told you he didn't mean it." Heronimous said, turning to Gabby.

"Well, perhaps he half meant it," Gabrial suggested.

"Yeah!" Sonny Joe agreed trying to get in their good books. "Because if I'd wanted to be unkind, I could have told him that the dark was full of monsters!"

"Yes, well..." Heronimous said dubiously.

Dwarfaun Gabrial whispered mysteriously into Hero's ear, "Don't forget Mandwarf."

"I know!" Heronimous said impatiently. "Anyway, you're in luck," he told Sonny Joe, "Mandwarf has a job for you."

"Oh," he perked up, "what sort of a job?"

"You'll find out," Heronimous told him, darkly.

The two Dwarfauns uncovered their Rhymestone and chanted together:

"Eeny Meeny Macaraca,
Alabaca Turiac…a tooth of a Tiger,
A Dragonfly's Scowl,
Human turn into… an OWL!"

In a flash Sonny Joe was a beautiful, snowy-white owl, with soft, sleek feathers and sturdy legs, strong, sharp talons, and a magnificent, hooked beak.

"This is more like it!" thought Sonny Joe and to his delight he discovered he could actually swivel his head right round in a full circle to admire himself all over.

"All right!" Heronimous said impatiently. "That's enough of that. Now pay attention. You must stop your Collie dog from chasing flying insects."

"Harry the Girl Dog?" asked Sonny Joe.

"She chases the bees, and snaps at all the other insects. They say that she might have killed a Queen Bee, the highest form of insect," said Gabrial.

"She's been a pet in your family for far too long," Heronimous added. "She's becoming almost as bad as a human. She pretends that she can't hear us."

"Perhaps she can't," Gabrial suggested. "Perhaps she's been listening to human voices for so long she's got …Humanitis."

"That's why Mandwarf wants you to talk to her before she goes after birds and animals," said Heronimous, "she might just listen to you."

"I can try," Sonny Joe said dubiously. "Only what do I say to her?"

"Why do you think we've turned you into an owl?" Heronimous asked crossly. "Owls are supposed to be wise. Prove it."

And with that the two Dwarfauns floated up into the soft evening air and off towards the apple tree, quickly becoming lost against the golden sunset. Sonny Joe felt envious.

"It must be wonderful to fly," he thought. Then he remembered. He was an owl! A bird! He could fly! He jumped upwards, beating his wings against the air and the pull of the earth at the same time. He flapped them again with rapid strokes of enormous power which seemed as effortless as putting one foot in front of the other. And with a surge of joy and pride he realised that he was, truly, airborne. He was flying!

Gracefully, he climbed through the air to the top of a tall Scots pine which overlooked the cottage, and alighted on a branch on one feathered leg, rather like the fairy on top of a Christmas tree. The short flight had been one of the most exhilarating experiences of his entire life and he was for a moment almost grateful that he had met the Dwarfauns who had made it possible.

Suddenly from below he heard familiar barking. With a jolt, Sonny Joe remembered why he had been turned into an owl, and what he had to do.

Harry the Girl Dog was chasing madly around the garden, barking and snapping at low-flying insects. Opening his broad wings, Sonny Joe took off and dived down in one long, gliding swoop towards Harry. For good measure he called, "You TWIT-TWOO!" as he skimmed just above her ears.

Startled, Harry looked up. "Boot of a binman!" she exclaimed. "What was that for?"

"Oh, you can hear me then," said Sonny Joe, as he came to rest on the sundial.

"Of course I can hear you," Harry said, in an indignant sort of way, "but who are you?"

"A friend, so listen. Your behaviour must change. Don't ever chase insects again. I know it's just a game to you," said Sonny Joe Owl, "but it isn't much of a game to them, and if you hadn't been a city dog for so long, you'd know that."

"Get away," said Harry. "They love it."

"You might think so," said Sonny Joe, "but have you ever asked them? So just lie down a minute and pay attention, I'm going to tell you a story."

Reluctantly, Harry the Girl Dog lay down on the grass, put her chin on her paws and made her ears droop.

A mild sense of panic gripped Sonny Joe because he realised he hadn't the faintest idea what story to tell.

"Once upon a time," he began...Harry the Girl Dog yawned noisily... "there was a pet dog rather like you, who belonged to some people called... Smith. The dog's name was...er...Scampidogs. The Smiths didn't have any children, so he was even more spoilt than you are and was never told off, not even when he barked at the postman and tried to bite him every morning." Sonny Joe struggled.

"Lucky beast," Harry said, enviously.

"And the game he liked most of all was chasing the birds and insects in the garden, trying to catch them..."

"Naturally," said Harry. "Who wouldn't?"

"Don't interrupt," said Sonny Joe sternly. "One day the Smiths found the dead body of a young blackbird in the garden. They couldn't believe that their Scampidogs could have done this, so they blamed the cat next door even though next door didn't even have a cat!

But all the other animals and birds and insects knew exactly who had done it, and from that day on none of them would ever go in his garden... except for one.

You see, the dead blackbird had a twin brother who vowed to take revenge. So everyday the twin blackbird flew into the Smiths' garden and waited for Scampidogs to be let out. Then he'd sit on a branch, just out of Scampidogs' reach, and start to nag at the dog...chirp-chirp, cheep-cheep, chitter-chatter-chitter-chatter...non-stop all day long, until Scampidogs couldn't stand the nagging any more and he'd actually bark to be let in again. It went on, day after day after day, month after month. The dog tried every trick in the book (and out of it) to catch the bird, but it was always too quick for him.

Finally, when he was very old, Scampidogs pleaded with the bird to stop and forgive him for having killed his brother. But the blackbird refused. So Scampidogs died, worn out by the blackbird's non-stop scolding, and only then did the other wildlife return to the garden. So there you are," Sonny Joe concluded.

"I don't believe a word of it," Harry said, but there was a kind of unhappy snuffle in her voice.

"You carry on the way you've been doing, and you'll find out," Sonny Joe Owl warned.

There was a long silence."It was only a game," she muttered.

"That's what Scampidogs used to say," Sonny Joe told her. "Only hurting other creatures isn't really very much fun, is it?" Harry didn't reply. "So will you leave the birds, insects and all the other little animals alone from now on?"

"Providing they leave me alone," Harry sighed. "But if they buzz all around my head I'll bark and snap as much as I like."

"It's a deal. If they don't annoy you, you won't terrorise them?" Sonny Joe confirmed.

Harry agreed and raising her tail in a gesture of proud independence, turned back to the cottage.

Sonny Joe Owl felt so pleased with himself that he took off from the sundial and went for a celebration flight.

For the first time since meeting the Dwarfauns he felt a sense of progress, and it was so exhilarating that he wanted to climb and soar for sheer joy.

He eventually turned and glided for home, feeling the wind rushing through his feathers. Because they were especially soft and allowed the wind through he was almost completely silent. Indeed, so silent was he that he spotted the waiting Dwarfauns below the climbing frame long before they saw him, and when he landed on a rung just above their heads he gave them both quite a shock.

"Argh!" said Heronimous crossly. "You could have said twit-twoo or something!"

"Sorry," said Sonny Joe. "I didn't realise you hadn't seen me."

"Yes you did!" said Heronimous, even more crossly. "When are you going to learn that you can't lie to a Dwarfaun?"

"Mandwarf, Hero," Gabrial whispered to his friend.

"Yes, yes, all right!" Heronimous shouted and stamped his little feet with rage. Turning back to the owl, he said menacingly, "Mandwarf wants to see you."

"Why?" thought Sonny Joe, panicking. "What have I done now?"

CHAPTER 5

Sonny Joe Owl expected to be taken somewhere special for his first meeting with Mandwarf, so it was a surprise when Hero and Gabby just stood there, ramrod straight, like soldiers standing to attention.

"Where is he?" Sonny Joe asked eagerly.

"Right here," said a voice.

As Sonny Joe looked in the direction of the voice there appeared before him a tiny boy, with a silvery covered top half of his body, a donkey tail with a rabbit bobtail, and little horns which grew out of his head, like the Dwarfauns, but who looked more human.

"Hello," he said. "I'm Mandwarf."

"Hello," said Sonny Joe.

"You've done very well. We're pleased with you. Aren't we, Hero?"

"Hummph!" said Heronimous.

"He's still not convinced that you've learnt your lesson," said Mandwarf.

"Oh, but I have!" cried Sonny Joe. "Honestly. Lots of them!"

"Yes," said Mandwarf. "I think you probably have."

"So please, can I go back to being a boy again, now?" Sonny Joe Owl asked.

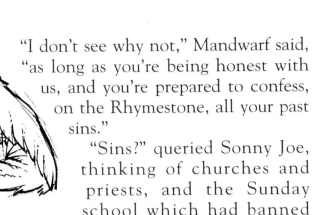

"I don't see why not," Mandwarf said, "as long as you're being honest with us, and you're prepared to confess, on the Rhymestone, all your past sins."

"Sins?" queried Sonny Joe, thinking of churches and priests, and the Sunday school which had banned him for letting off stink bombs in the middle of the hymns.

"No, not those sort of sins," Mandwarf explained, "sins against Nature. Things that you have done during your brief human existence that you now know to have been wrong, according to the lessons that you say you have learnt."

Sonny Joe dug deep into his memory. "I did once throw a brick into a wasps' nest," he confessed.

"Right. Now hold the Rhymestone," Mandwarf commanded. Heronimous and Gabrial ceremoniously unwrapped the magic stone from its protective clothing and rested it upon Sonny Joe's outstretched wings.

"Begin again," said Mandwarf.

"I once threw a brick into a wasps' nest," Sonny Joe repeated.

An amazing thing happened.

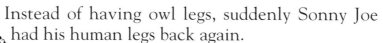

Instead of having owl legs, suddenly Sonny Joe had his human legs back again.

"Go on," Mandwarf said.

"When Mum wasn't looking once, I did put a worm in Josh's spaghetti," Sonny Joe admitted.

Instantly his body was no longer that of an owl, but his own tall boy's body once more. Now there were only his wings and his head to go, and Sonny Joe had never felt more like confessing all his sins in his whole life.

"I'm ashamed to admit it," he said, "but sometimes, when I was with my city friends, we'd catch cats and swing them round by their tails."

The instant he had finished speaking, the Rhymestone was no longer resting on his outstretched wings, but in his hands at the ends of his own, outstretched, arms. Eagerly, he tried to think of the next awful thing he could confess to. But then, to his dismay, he realised that he couldn't think of anything else that was cruel.

"Go on," said Mandwarf.

"I can't think of anything," Sonny Joe faltered.

"Oh dear," said Mandwarf. "And you were doing so well."

"What about trying to tear the wings off that butterfly?" Heronimous demanded.

"Of course!" Sonny Joe gasped. How could he have forgotten the

one incident that had landed him in all this trouble. "Thank you."

"Too late, I'm afraid," said Mandwarf. "You can't be prompted by us. You have to think of these things and confess them yourself, or the magic doesn't work."

Sonny Joe dropped the Rhymestone and touched his head.

"Oh no, it's not fair!" he shouted, as he felt the soft, downy feathers and a sharp, hooked beak.

"What are we to do with you now?" Mandwarf continued, looking up at Sonny Joe Owl-Head. "It looks as though you're going to have to stay in the Ringdom after all. We can't let you go with that head on."

"Oh, please!" cried Sonny Joe. "Can't you say a rhyme or something?"

"It's more complicated than you think," said Mandwarf. "Still, never mind," he continued breezily, "I'm sure you'll get to like it here eventually, I did."

"But I don't want to stay here!" cried Sonny Joe. " I can't stay here! Mum and Dad'll be going mad, worrying about where I've got to!"

"That's never seemed to bother you very much in the past," Mandwarf remarked, "so it's a bit late to start worrying about it now, because there's nothing we can do."

"But there MUST be," cried Sonny Joe.

Seeing how miserable and earnest he was, Mandwarf, Heronimous and Gabrial gathered together in a football huddle, whispering between themselves. Eventually they turned back to Sonny Joe.

"There is only one Being who can change you back to your full human form," Mandwarf told him. "And that is Queen Fairest Regal, our Supreme Fairy Being. But it depends on whether or not you survive the long, arduous and dangerous journey to reach the heart of the Inner Ringdom, through three Rungdoms to the top of the climbing frame ladder where Her Majesty lives."

Sonny Joe looked up at the top of the ladder. It didn't look so very long, or arduous, and certainly not all that dangerous. It was, after all, a journey he had been on thousands of times already as a boy.

"Come on, then," he said. "What are we waiting for?"

"Not so fast!" cried Mandwarf. "You're not in your own dimension now. This is Ringdom time and space. You must have guides to help you." And, turning to Heronimous and Gabrial, he solemnly assigned to them the task of accompanying Sonny Joe on this difficult journey.

Strapping two acorns onto each other's backs, one filled with cowslip milk, and the other with climbing gear, the two Dwarfauns bade farewell to Mandwarf, and led Sonny Joe to the rocks at the foot of the climbing frame ladder. Looking up at it now, it looked much higher than he remembered, and seemed to stretch up and up until it touched the sky.

"It's very tall," he observed.

"And very hazardous," Gabrial agreed, "unless you know what you're doing."

Heronimous, meanwhile, was unloading a rope and grappling iron from Gabrial's

acorn. With great skill he threw it over the first rung
of the ladder. Beckoning to the others to follow, he
climbed swiftly up the rope like a seasoned mountain
climber. Gabrial helped Sonny Joe up, and soon all
three were safely on the first rung.

To Sonny Joe's astonishment, instead of the
gaping hole he expected to see down inside,
he discovered he was no longer on the rung
of a ladder, but on the edge of a cliff, and
that stretching away from them was a
landscape of trees and rich, green grass, all
bathed in bright sunlight.

"Come on," Heronimous chided him. "It's a
lot further than you know and if we don't get a
move on we'll never make it!"

Sonny Joe dutifully followed his Dwarfaun guides
across this magic landscape of the First Rungdom
but not before secretly jumping up and down to
make sure he didn't drop through into the Ringdom
below. Before long, he noticed that it was chilly
and the grass beneath their feet was turning into
snow.

"Don't worry," said Gabrial, "the higher, the
hotter."

"How weird," he thought, and trudged on in the wake
of his Dwarfaun guides, as the snow deepened and
the air grew colder. Even stranger, was that

behind them he could see only one set of footprints – his.

By now his feet were getting wet and his legs tired. He had heard of people falling asleep in the snow, and never waking up again. Snow was fun but not when all you were wearing was a light summer t-shirt, jeans and trainers! Sonny Joe didn't think he could go much further... when suddenly, out of the whiteness of the surrounding landscape, there loomed the second rung of the ladder.

"Up and over, Hero?" asked Gabrial.

Heronimous looked back at the floundering Sonny Joe to see how much strength he had left. "We'll have to, Gabby," he said. "We've come too far to go back, although he doesn't look in such good shape."

"Don't worry about me," assured Sonny Joe. "I'm all right."

"I should hope so," Heronimous told him, "we're only here for your sake."

So saying, the Dwarfauns held hands and slowly floated up into the air until they were standing high on the edge of the next Rungdom, looking down on the boy with the owl's head.

"Here, boy," said Hero, throwing down the rope.

His fingers numb with cold and his limbs heavy with tiredness, Sonny Joe slowly hauled himself up the rope after them. Eventually, he was able to roll over the edge and lie, gasping in the hot sunshine that now greeted him. "I'd hate to be the fairy Weather Forecaster," he panted.

"We're never going to get there at this rate," Heronimous muttered.

"I don't understand it," Sonny Joe gasped to Gabrial. "Never mind the weird weather, how come when I'm so big and you're so small, you don't seem to get tired at all?"

"That's because you make the same mistake all humans make," Gabrial told him. "You confuse small with weak, whereas we're actually much stronger than you humans." And to prove his point, the tiny Dwarfaun bent down, grasped Sonny Joe's leg with one hand and bodily lifted him from the ground as though he was a branch of dead wood.

"Wow!" shouted Sonny Joe. "That's incredible."

"Easy peazy," said Gabrial. And feeling a little light-hearted, he decided to sing a Ringdom Rhyme to the boy:

"We're no fools, cos the Ringdom rules
And the Ringdom rules for good
Our fairy ways, turn night to days,
But that's all understood.

We've got time, cos the Ringdom rhymes
And the Ringdom rhymes this way
Our fairy tails turn boys to snails
And back again today."

"Enough of that," badgered Heronimous. "We're running out of time!"

CHAPTER 6

Remembering the seriousness of their quest, Gabrial gently placed Sonny Joe back on the ground, and the three of them continued on their way across a land of lush tropical vegetation, with long snake-like vines, and rainbow coloured waterfalls, falling silently into cool, swirling whirlpools.

As they walked over carpets of exotic flowers, shoals of silver flying fish jumped in and out of the water, and as they strolled past orchards of ripe pineapples, mangos, paw-paws and giant strawberries, flocks of unbelievably pretty macaws passed overhead in flying formation.

It was such a beautiful place that Sonny Joe wanted to stay awhile. Yet onwards and upwards they had to go. When they finally reached the third rung, he realised that, strangely, the higher they climbed, the hotter it became.

The Third Rungdom was a land of overheated sand dunes, which led down to the sea. If they hadn't been able to paddle in the water to cool themselves, the heat would have been unbearable.

"Where are we now?" asked Sonny Joe, wiping the sweat from his beak.

"This is the third and final rung before we reach the top of the climbing frame," Gabrial informed him. "Once we're across here, we only have to climb the final rung, and your full humanity will be at hand, in the heart of the Inner Ringdom."

"But be warned," said Heronimous. "This is probably the hardest Rungdom of all to cross."

"So first," said Gabrial, "we will share our cowslip milk to give us sustenance."

Although the rich, white liquid was sweet and satisfying, there wasn't an awful lot of it, and when the last drop was gone, Sonny Joe still felt horribly empty inside. He wished he had stopped to pick and eat some of the luscious fruits growing in the last Rungdom, for the land they were now in was so hot and barren it was like a desert.

They headed inland, leaving behind the cooling wash of the waves. The hot sand began to burn Sonny Joe's feet, through the soles of his trainers. The blazing sun beat down remorselessly. Just to complete his misery, a sudden sandstorm blew up, whipping the sand into his large yellow eyes. Battling on, head down, through this stinging blizzard, he could feel the strength steadily ebbing out of his legs, and leaden, weary weakness take its place. It wasn't only the effects of the sun and sand but also that of hunger and thirst.

"If I don't get something to eat soon," he shouted to the two Dwarfauns, "I think I'll faint."

No sooner had he said this than through the sandstorm appeared a tall, old woman with sand coloured hair, wearing a sandy coloured cloak, and on the end of her long, broken nose, were delicately balanced two sandglasses. On her thin, sunburnt feet she wore leather-thonged sandals and, from one bony shoulder, hung a sandbag. You might have said that the old woman was entirely made of sand. Of immediate interest to Sonny Joe, however, was the fact that she was holding out... a sandwich.

"Who are you?" he asked.

"Don't talk to her!" cried Gabrial. "It's the Sand Witch. You mustn't listen to her!"

"Here, young man," the Sand Witch called, in a voice that was like the shivering of the sands. "A sandwich for you, a real sandwich, made of the finest sand by the kindest, cleverest Sand Witch."

"Oh, thank you," said Sonny Joe. "Food at last."

"Don't take it unless you want to be a Sandman for evermore!" Heronimous warned.

"A Sandman?" Sonny Joe asked, somewhat confused.

"The Sandmen live with the Sand Witch in a sandcastle at Sandringham by the Sea," Heronimous explained. "They were mortals once who made the mistake of sampling a Sand Witch sandwich and now they float round in the Dream State, sprinkling nightmares into the pleasant dreams of children."

"Vicious lies," hissed the Sand Witch in her voice of sinking sand. "Here, young man, I made this sandwich just for you."

"Don't touch it!" Heronimous ordered.

"Oh please," Sonny Joe begged him. "If only you knew how hungry I am!"

"Trust us or be doomed!" Heronimous cried.

"If you insist," said the sad, starving Sonny Joe. Turning to the Sand Witch he said, "thank you for the offer, but I'd better not, if you don't mind."

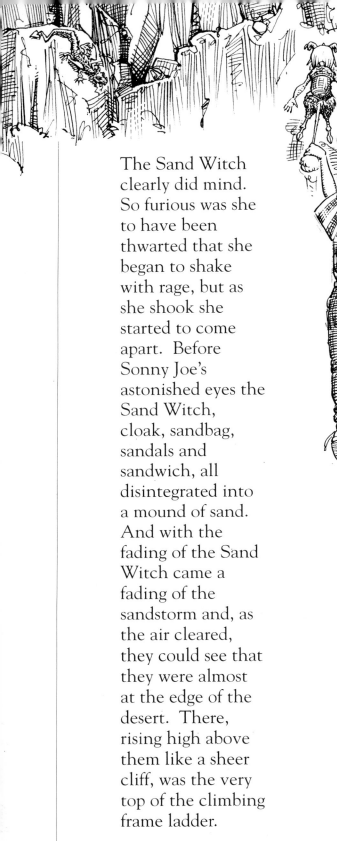

The Sand Witch clearly did mind. So furious was she to have been thwarted that she began to shake with rage, but as she shook she started to come apart. Before Sonny Joe's astonished eyes the Sand Witch, cloak, sandbag, sandals and sandwich, all disintegrated into a mound of sand. And with the fading of the Sand Witch came a fading of the sandstorm and, as the air cleared, they could see that they were almost at the edge of the desert. There, rising high above them like a sheer cliff, was the very top of the climbing frame ladder.

"Oh, no! I'm never going to be able to climb that!" cried the exhausted Sonny Joe.

The two Dwarfauns looked at each other.

"We could 'up and over' him," Gabrial suggested.

Heronimous gave a resigned sort of nod. Turning to Sonny Joe, he said, "Hold our tails. But whatever you do, DON'T look down."

Sonny Joe did as he was told and took hold of the Dwarfaun's tails. Gently they rose up into the air as though they were on an invisible escalator. Now, whereas Sonny Joe Owl had felt completely at home soaring on the wind, Sonny Joe Boy, with only an owl head and no wings, felt decidedly strange with nothing beneath him except air. Nearing the top, Sonny Joe was just starting to get used to the sensation, when he forgot Heronimous' warning and... looked down.

Instantly, his weightlessness left him. Like a lump of lead, he fell down, down through the air, dragging Heronimous and Gabrial with him. He was completely unable to let go of their tails, and down they floated, like slow motion skydivers, plummeting silently to

their certain deaths.

"You looked down!" Heronimous shouted angrily.

"I'm sorry!" Sonny Joe shouted back, as the jagged rocks at the foot of the Rungdom cliff rushed to meet them. "Honestly! I'm sorry about everything! I'm sorry I was so bone-headed stubborn. I'm sorry I was so ignorant and cruel. I'm sorry I hurt that butterfly."

Hardly had these final words escaped his mouth when a large shadow swooped beneath them, and their whole world turned topsy-turvy. Sonny Joe and the Dwarfauns had landed on something solid and found themselves drifting upwards on the velvet wings of a giant butterfly.

CHAPTER 7

Instead of the bone-crushing rocks below, the top of the climbing frame now rushed towards them. They just cleared the last rung of the ladder and, for a moment, Sonny Joe thought they were about to keep going all the way into outer space. Luckily soft, fluffy clouds slowed them down. Secure on the strong, broad wings of the butterfly, all the terror of the fall was taken away and when they tumbled through the white mist into brilliant sunshine, their fears floated away with the clouds.

Below them was an oasis of rich, golden sand, and a lagoon of sparkling, silvery water, surrounded by tall palm trees. Gathered in a circle on the banks of the lagoon was a huge assembly of Fairy Beings. Sonny Joe, Heronimous and Gabrial gently floated into the centre of the gathering, landing with the merest bump on the soft golden sand, which Sonny Joe was astonished to find was gold dust.

He looked around and spotted Mandwarf sitting on a large, glittering cut-glass rock at the water's edge.

"Well done, Sonny Joe," Mandwarf smiled at him. "Although you do tend to leave things to the last moment, I hope you realise that because you finally recanted all your wickedness you were saved by one of our largest Peacock Eye butterflies. If you had not, you would surely have been dashed to pieces at the bottom of the cliff, taking Heronimous and Gabrial with you. But in your moment of terror you were totally honest with yourself, and so you are here, in the heart of the Inner Ringdom. And look who has consented to meet you."

Mandwarf pointed to the centre of the silvery lagoon, and there, standing on the water was the most beautiful Fairy Being you could imagine.

She was dressed in a long, diaphanous, shimmering white gown, edged with tiny, white seed-pearls which complemented her pale complexion. Tiny stars glistened in her flowing, white-blonde hair. On her head was a crown of golden buttercups. On her snow white feet were golden rings, one on each tiny toe. All around her was a shimmering glow, and from her flowed the feeling of absolute peace and serenity. Sonny Joe had no need to ask who this dazzling creature was. He knew she was Queen Fairest Regal.

"Sonny Joseph Jones," she whispered, in a voice that was clearly heard by all her Fairy subjects. "My senior advisers have told me that while in the bodies of various creatures, you have at last come to terms with Nature, and have started to help animals and humans alike. You are thus worthy to be returned unto humanity.

You will find that days, months, and years here in our Ringdom are but seconds, minutes and hours in your own dimension. In time you will even find that your memory of what has happened here may grow faint or disappear altogether. But remember this: if you ever forget the

58

lessons learnt in the Ringdom, and you intentionally harm or kill any insect, bird or animal, you will instantly be transformed into that same insect, bird or animal. Do you understand?"

"Yes," replied Sonny Joe without hesitation.

"Then you may proceed, Mandwarf," said the Queen.

Mandwarf clapped his hands twice, then proclaimed:

"Heronimous Bosh and Gabrial Bone
Deliver to us the Ringdom Rhymestone."

Heronimous and Gabrial, who were also in awe of the Queen, shuffled forward with the precious Rhymestone and placed it at Sonny Joe's feet.

"Bring it to me," commanded the Queen from the middle of the lagoon.

At first, Sonny Joe thought that she was speaking to Hero and Gabby, but he then realised that the entire company was looking at him.

"But I can't walk on water!" he whispered, out of the corner of his mouth to Mandwarf.

The Fairy Queen who could clearly hear over long distances just as easily as she could speak, gave a laugh that was like the ripple of a harp's strings. "Don't be afraid," she said, "trust me. Come."

So, picking up the Rhymestone, Sonny Joe stepped out onto the water.

His feet didn't even break the surface. He felt as if he were gliding. It was like skating on ice, yet he had no fear

of falling. Indeed, as he drew nearer to the Fairy Queen he felt calmer than he had ever felt in his life.

"Place the Rhymestone before me," the Queen told him. "Now stand upon it."

Sonny Joe did so, no longer even amazed that he and the Rhymestone did not sink.

Turning to the assembled throng on the bank, the Queen said, "And now, fellow beings of the Inner Ringdom, all join together and let us send this boy back to humanity."

Bowing their heads, the Fairy Beings all joined hands, tails or wings and with one voice they began to chant:

> *"Eeny Meeny Macaraca*
> *Alabaca Turiac …a start of a New Life,*
> *An End to all Vanity*
> *Sonny Joe return … to Humanity!"*

As the brightest ever glow of light bathed the lagoon and the heart of the Inner Ringdom, Sonny Joe felt the Rhymestone starting to dissolve under his feet. Ever so slowly he sank into the molten, silvery waters of the lagoon. As the waters closed over his head he was just able to hear:

> "*Eeny Meeny Macaraca*
> *Alabaca Turiac … Animal Magic*
> *And Insects all Seeing,*
> *Turn Sonny Joe … into a HUMAN BEING!*"

He raised one arm to wave goodbye, to Queen Fairest Regal, to Mandwarf, and to Heronimous and Gabrial...

...and that was how he found himself, in the centre of the climbing frame in the garden of Sunset Cottage. He had one arm raised, and he was waving to his parents who were watching him from the house. In his other hand he was holding his school blazer, and, trapped within it, was the Peacock Eye butterfly.

"Oh no!" he thought. "How could I? What have I done? Please, please don't let it be hurt ..."

Gently he opened his blazer and the butterfly, apparently none the worse for its brief imprisonment, stretched its wings and fluttered off in the warm sunlight towards the flowers at the end of the garden . . .

THE END